AMERICAN SQUIRE

SIERRA SIMONE

1

F ew of us are lucky enough to know a real wizard.

Even fewer of us are lucky enough to be sent on a quest by one.

Or at least that's what I tell myself during my endless flight from D.C. to London, and during the following train ride to Exeter, and during the long, harrowing drive while I struggle not to scrape my rental car against the hedgerows while I consult the GPS on my phone.

I squint at the screen and then sigh.

Somehow it's taken me an entire hour just to make it fourteen miles.

I sigh again, as if hedges and sheep are Google's fault, and then toss the phone on the passenger seat. Supposedly, I'm only a short drive through a village away, but I didn't get much sleep on the plane, and everything is starting to feel blearily unreal. I've kind of given up hope that Thornchapel exists at all by this point.

All this way for a book, I think tiredly.

If the request for help hadn't come from Merlin *and* Nimue—Merlin's new . . . well, his new whatever she is—I might have said no.

The president I'd served faithfully for four years is dead, and while his successor offered me the same job, I couldn't accept it. It feels too close to moving on, and I don't want to move on. Not yet, not when I still feel so wrong inside, so ruined and lost.

But when Nimue asked me to help her and Merlin, I felt a flicker of the old Belvedere. The Belvedere who could do anything and do it in trendy glasses and a smile. I said yes before I even realized I'd opened my mouth.

I nudge the car over a bridge and into a village called Thorncombe that looks like it's been pulled straight off a postcard. It features a stone church with a square Norman tower, an accompanying graveyard with weathered tombstones, and plenty of pubs in adorably sagging buildings. It's only a few days before Christmas, and everything is hung with wreaths and ribbons and garlands, and it looks like one of those miniature Christmas villages my grandma likes to collect. I normally don't enjoy things this transparently festive, but it's strangely heartwarming to see the village all cozy and cheerful in the middle of the cold, brown wastes of the moors.

There's no such coziness or cheer at Thornchapel itself.

After a sharp turn and a trip over a small ice-snaggled river, I creep down the long driveway until I encounter a stern edifice that looks older than the hills themselves.

Crenellations chew at the winter sky like stone teeth, and the windows reflect back trees and trees and trees. It's three stories of gray stone, asymmetrical and obviously added to over time, and there are no wreaths here, no Christmas tree beaming merrily through the front window. In a way, the lack of seasonal cheer is a relief, since there's a possibility I'll be staying here over the holiday and I'd hate to feel like I'm imposing on the Guest family, whom I'm told owns the estate. No, there's just a house, and a book inside this house that's been promised to Merlin and that is therefore my job to find.

I park behind a narrow work van, taking note of the signs of renovation happening around the house—a big construction dumpster tucked discreetly around one side, a bucket of paint propping open the massive wooden door at the front—and then go to retrieve my suitcase from the trunk just as a sleek Audi pulls into the driveway behind me. I close the trunk lid and turn, wondering if this is the family lawyer, Mr. Cremer, who I've spoken briefly on the phone with.

But when the car shuts off and its owner climbs out looking like a *GQ* cover, I know he can't be Mr. Cremer. I've worked in D.C. for four years, and every lawyer I know looks like he's on stimulants or blood pressure medication—or both. This man looks cold and fit and serene; a block of ice that's been carved into a god shape, clad in a bespoke suit, and then covered in one of those expensive wool coats.

(You know the kind: dark and long, and fitted just enough to make you want to slide your hands underneath it.)

Paired with a gray scarf, nice gloves, and burnished leather shoes, he exudes cool elegance and sophistication; he radiates the kind of remote power I can't help but crave like an addict.

And his face—*that face*. I stop moving just to stare at it. Pale and striking, with high graven cheekbones and a haughty mouth. He's got pearl-gray eyes, dark hair with just a breath of silver at the temples, and an expression of pure imperial arrogance as he gazes at Thornchapel. He's Caesar standing at the Rubicon, Hannibal gazing up at the Alps. It's an expression that says he's ready to conquer, and conquer ruthlessly.

I imagine that look directed at *me*, and heat arrows down my spine. What would it be like to be the object of his merciless determination? What would it be like to have that leather-gloved hand gripping my jaw as he forces his cock down my throat?

Hoping he can't see the heat in my face or the thickening behind my zipper, I give him a smile.

And all I get is a slight nod in return.

A couple of months ago, this would have barely registered. My job was to keep the President of the United States comfortable, informed and on task—hourly I had to face down pissy senators, angry diplomats, and worst of all, the personal aides of other world leaders. It took a lot more than a cold nod to put a dent in my smile.

But now, with Maxen Ash Colchester dead and with me drifting from place to place with no direction and no purpose—well, this beautiful man's dismissal of me feels like another glum nudge from the universe, reminding me that nothing matters and nothing ever will.

My master is dead, and I'll never get to serve again.

2

As promised by the dumpster and construction supplies, the inside of the house is a mess, which I can see even through my fogged-up glasses. Me and the wool-coated Ice God are welcomed by the real Mr. Cremer, a tall, reedy man with rimless glasses, who shows us to our rooms and tells us that the owner of the house will be joining us for dinner.

"I'm happy to take possession of the book any time, Mr. Cremer," I say, a bit hopefully, as he walks us both down to the ground floor to give us a tour. "I hate to be a burden."

"Nonsense," Mr. Cremer says. "Mr. Guest is delighted to have you here. I'm certain he'll want to hear all your stories about working in the White House. And besides . . ."

We're walking through a narrow corridor lined with arched windows to get to the library. It looks like something out of a monastery, as do the iron-bound doors set into the stone wall, and when Mr. Cremer pushes them open, even the Ice God next to me lets out a startled breath. Before us is the library in *Beauty and the Beast*, if *Beauty and the Beast* were set in the austere gloom of the seventeenth century. There's countless books on sturdy, endless bookshelves, two stories of it all with plenty of ladders and clever little staircases to connect them. All the light comes from a large bank of two-story windows at the end, and the only ornamentation is the carved wood and the varied colors of the books themselves. The ceiling is so high and the room so deep that shadows curl like big cats in the corner, even in daylight.

"The library is rather big," Mr. Cremer states, in the bland tones of obvious understatement. "It might take you some time to find the book Merlin is looking for."

The ice god has wandered inside the library, but he's not gazing at the shelves with the slack-jawed wonder I am. He's assessing everything with a cold, calculating gaze. Every now and again, he pulls a book off the shelf to examine its condition.

His efficiency and dismissive contempt of unworthy items is powerfully erotic. I have no idea why.

"Who is he?" I whisper-ask to the lawyer.

"Ah, yes. That's Sidney Blount," the lawyer replies. "From the auction house. He's here to catalog the Guests' artwork in anticipation of it being sold off."

Sidney Blount. It sounded like a war name to me, or maybe something out of a 1930s pulp story about a soul-deadened detective who's forgotten how to feel anything but bitterness and lust.

As opposed to *Ryan Belvedere*, which is a name that sounds happy and dutiful—at least it does to me.

Or at least it did.

"Mr. Blount doesn't mind working this close to the holiday?" I ask, trying to push away from unhappy thoughts and move on to something else.

Mr. Cremer gives the world's smallest one-shouldered shrug, so subtle I barely catch it. "Mr. Blount's company stands to earn a substantial amount of money from this. And my client is eager to dispatch of the artwork—it was important to his father, and so Mr. Guest is compelled to remove it from the house."

Even though Mr. Cremer's tone of voice hasn't changed, I can tell he disapproves.

"I'm guessing his father is no longer alive?"

"Correct."

I think I can picture this Mr. Guest now, thin and sour and old, the kind of middle-aged man who pins all his dead dreams on his father . . . while making all the same choices his father did. I'm already dreading having to make conversation with him, but I remind myself that I've dealt with worse in the White House. I can handle the mulish petulance of an old man for a few days.

In the library, Sidney Blount is now leaning over a curio case with his hands folded behind his back. Without the wool coat, I can see how perfectly tailored his suit is, how it clings to the lean lines of his torso and hips. He's tall and broad-shouldered, and even though I place him at about ten years older than me, in his late thirties, there's plenty of muscle testing the seams of his shoulders and arms whenever he pulls something closer to get a better look.

"How do you know Merlin?" I ask Cremer. It's random, it's such a random thing to ask, but I feel like I've been staring at Sidney Blount long enough for it to be weird, and I don't want the lawyer to notice.

"We went to school together," Cremer answers. "We've kept in touch since then, and I help him look after some of his family's property here in the UK. When he reached out to me about that book, I was more than happy to talk to Mr. Guest about letting Merlin buy it from him. And as I expected, Mr. Guest said—and I quote—*he can have the whole damn library if he wants.* I, of course, advised against that."

Sidney strides back towards us, a haughty, well-dressed silhouette with the large windows behind him framing him in pale winter light.

"Does Mr. Guest want the items in these cases appraised as well?" Sidney asks.

His voice is so sharp and precise that I could use it to fold shirts. I could use it to cut myself.

I sigh. Longingly, quietly.

No one seems to notice.

"Just the paintings," Cremer replies.

"He should have all of this appraised," Sidney says, turning back to face the room. This close, I can see the faint lines around his eyes, and the barest shadow of stubble beginning to darken his jaw. I resist the urge to shiver again; my hunger for older men is insatiable. "Your client should bring someone in to see to this library before it rots away in neglect."

I expect Mr. Cremer to protest, but he only gives a defeated exhale. "Yes, I'll tell him."

Sidney doesn't acknowledge this—he doesn't seem like the type of man to acknowledge when people have agreed with him, as if he expects that as his due.

I also have a bit of a kink for that too, if I'm honest.

Cremer's phone rings, and excusing himself, he leaves to take it in the hallway, which means it's only me and Sidney left inside this moldering cathedral of books.

I take a step forward, peering into the deep recesses made by the shelves, and consider my task. I'm very good at what I do—or at least, I was very good at what I did, before my employer and king died and I didn't care about being good at anything anymore. Finding a book in a library should be no more difficult than getting a suit dry-cleaned with only an hour's notice or briefing the President on a day's packed schedule while we both jog across the tarmac to catch the car.

It doesn't take me long to assess the layout of the library, and not much longer than that to go through a flow-chart of options in my head about the best way to approach the search. A job well done is accomplished in the planning as much as in the execution, and even if I'm not technically being paid, even if this job doesn't affect anyone but Merlin and Nimue, it matters to me to do it well.

There's a prickle of something at the back of my neck, hot and light all at once, and I look back at the doors just in time to see Sidney Blount looking away from me.

3

Years of sleeping only when the President slept—and often less —mean that I'm fairly energized after a two-hour nap, even with the jet lag. I shave and shower, change into a pair of chinos and a leaf-green sweater that sets off my olive complexion, and then I spend an embarrassing amount of time fussing with my hair.

Before, in my life working for Ash, there was no time for vanity and there was no bandwidth for fashion. I had my roster of tweedy clothes, my trusty glasses, and I'm blessed with a thick flop of black hair that looks good no matter what I do. But thinking about sitting down at the table with the meticulous Sidney Blount, a man who scoffs at rare books and glares at Roman artifacts inside glass cases, has me worried that I'll look immature or foppish or vain.

But there's no helping it. The hair must flop, and I don't have the right tools to manage it. I arrange it as tamely as I can—not very— and head downstairs to dinner, where I'm greeted by Mr. Cremer and a handsome young man in his early twenties.

"You must be Ryan Belvedere," the young man says, extending his hand with a grin. He's got a flop of hair to rival mine and hazel eyes like windows to summer in the midst of all this cold and damp. And his smile has an uneven hitch on one side of his upper lip, roguish and innocent all at the same time, the grin of a young man just on the verge, just at the threshold. In another year, maybe in another handful of months, he won't be a comely youth but a man in the first flush of his power.

And that's not at all my type, given my penchant for older, crueler men, but my heart speeds up all the same as our hands touch.

"Mr. Belvedere," Cremer says, "this is Auden Guest, your host."

This is Auden Guest? I try to hide my shock as I shake his hand in return and then nod my agreement to his gesture at the open wine bottle nearby. I really thought I was staying at the house of a splotchy, book-hating, father-blaming miser, but nope. Just a gorgeous boy with hazel eyes and an open, crooked smile.

"Thank you so much for allowing me to stay here," I say as I accept the glass of wine. Our fingertips brush, and while it's not sheer electricity between us, I still feel my cheeks warm. It's been over a year since I've touched another person with more than the most perfunctory of courtesies, and even the punishments I'd come to crave at my local kink club were too hard to seek out between the hectic pace of Ash's re-election campaign and then my grief after his assassination. I'm starved for caresses and slaps both, and tonight is the first time I've really felt it, felt the hunger and the lack.

Maybe Thornchapel is stirring me awake again. Urging me back to life.

I look up to see Sidney Blount in the doorway of the dining room, staring at me and Auden Guest. His expression is hard and cold, his eyes are like ice under a flat sky, and suddenly I know that if he snapped his fingers right now, I'd drop to my knees. Right here in the dining room, here in front of everyone. I wouldn't even set down my wine first, I wouldn't even mind dropping it in my haste to obey him, in the hopes that he'd make me lick every spilled drop off the rug. That he'd punish me for the insult to my host.

Then Sidney glances away, stepping in with his hands in his pockets and a line between his eyebrows as he no doubt catalogs the antique furniture in the room.

There's a difference between cruel and just plain not interested, Ryan, I remind myself. The former is one of my favorite things in the world, and the latter is something I won't hurt myself with ever again. I've already spent the last four years quietly aching for the two most powerful men in my country as I watched them ache after each other —there's no sense in starting an even more hopeless attachment to someone I barely know.

But I still can't stop my eyes from drifting to him as we sit and a rosy-cheeked woman named Abby bustles in with our dinner. I can't stop watching him as he lifts his wineglass—by the stem, no unsightly smudges on Sidney Blount's glass, no sir—and as he tilts his head to listen to Cremer or Auden say this or that. As he eats with a precision that's as joyless as it is elegant.

"So Mr. Cremer tells me that you worked for the former President?" Auden asks after we've finished with our meal, and moved on to the little apple tarts Abby's brought in. "I'm so sorry about what happened, by the way."

"Thank you," I say. I've grown practiced at deflecting people's condolences, because there's simply no way to describe what Ash meant to me. It's easier to pretend that I lost a boss and not a king, it's easier to pretend I'm merely sad rather than completely purposeless, drifting without a master to serve.

Auden seems to sense that there's a conversational mire ahead and looks like he's about to change the subject, but Sidney pierces me with his gray eyes as he leans back and asks, "And what did you do for the President, Mr. Belvedere? What was your job, exactly?"

It's an easy question, Ryan, you can do this without crying.

In and out.

"I was President Colchester's personal aide," I say. "I was everything he needed to get through his day. I made sure he had his notes, the right clothes, the right speech, the right food. I woke him, fed him, fended off people who wanted his time; I led him and I followed him. I was—"

I break off, suddenly unable to find words. Not just the right words, but any words, all words. They're gone, completely gone in the face of what I was to a man who's now dead.

"You were his," Sidney finishes softly for me. He's studying me as one of his fingers rubs thoughtfully over the delicate gold paint on his coffee cup. "That's what you were. You were his."

I nod my head once, not trusting myself to answer.

"So you were like a valet?" Cremer asks. "An aide-de-camp?"

"Body man," Auden says suddenly, breaking into the conversation. "That's what they're called, yes? A body man."

I want to close my eyes against the rush of memories those words invoke, of the time Ash once used my body to soothe *his* man, his estranged lover Embry. Of all the times I wished he'd use my body to soothe himself, not because I was jealous of his wife or of his lover, but simply because I loved him so much that I wanted to give him everything. I worshipped him as my hero, I venerated him as my saint, and I would have stopped at nothing to ease his burdens.

"You were like a squire of old," Sidney says. "Tending to a king."

A squire. I like that. I like the feel of it in my mind, laden with images of pennants and armor. It sounds more romantic, more weighty than *aide* or *assistant*.

"Yes, like a squire," I agree.

"And you didn't find the work ignoble at all?" Sidney presses, his finger still tracing the filigreed patterns of his cup. "It wasn't demeaning?"

It's an unkind question, and Sidney wields it like scalpel—but strangely, it feels good. Like he's slicing through something sticky and confining to let in the air.

All the same, my temper rouses the slightest bit. "There's no such thing as ignoble work," I say. "There's nothing inherently less dignifying about compiling notes and running errands than writing poetry or crab-fishing or curating a museum. Yes, I was a squire, a body man. But my work meant that a great man could do *his* work, which I believed in. I was of service, I was essential, and I made life better and easier and more worthwhile for a man I cared deeply about—and *that* is noble to me."

The table stares at me, all of them quiet in the face of my heated response. Cremer looks a little embarrassed on my behalf at my outburst, and Auden has his pretty forehead wrinkled in thought, but Sidney Blount looks . . . pleased?

"So for me, there's no shame in small jobs," I continue. I ignore the spike of heat in my belly at seeing approval in Sidney's gaze. "There's only shame in jobs poorly done."

"It must have been hard to work with someone so closely and then lose him," Cremer offers, obviously trying to restore the equilibrium of the conversation.

"Yes," I reply, feeling tired and weak and sad. "Yes, it was."

"And what will you do next?" Sidney presses again. "Where will you go? Whom will you serve?"

It should have been an odd choice of words, even for a former personal aide, but to me they aren't odd at all. *Serve* has the cadence of sweet music to me, the harp of David soothing Saul, the whispered percussion of a sleeping king, able to sleep soundly because his servant is keeping watch, and so the answer comes out before I can even consider what it is I want to say.

"If I serve again, it will be my choice. And God willing, it will be for a long, long time."

4

Morning comes with silvery light and a fussy wind, and when I pad over to the windows in my bedroom, I see snowflakes big as feathers fluttering past the glass. I watch them for a minute, as the flakes catch on the branches of the trees and the shrubs, and on my windowsill. There's something rather cozy about it, knowing I don't have to go anywhere, knowing there are no errands to run in the slush and slick of it all. All I have to do is find a nice cup of coffee and dig through a library—I mean, people pay their own money to do that, and here I am on Merlin's dime, with a genial host and a job to accomplish. And having a job to accomplish is one of my favorite things in the world.

I get dressed with more anticipation than I've felt in weeks, pulling on jeans and a thick shawl-collared sweater over a *Reading Rainbow* T-shirt, running a pointless hand through my stupid hair, and then donning my signature glasses. I skip my usual shave because I'm feeling a little indulgent with the snow, and it's not a privilege I ever had working in the White House.

Auden told me last night to make free with the kitchen, but I'm not a breakfast person, so I just make some coffee in the French press while I watch the snow and then head to the library, feeling deeply rested despite the early hour. It's a few hours later than I normally sleep, since I needed to wake around four or five most days to get things ready for Ash, and I slept like the dead last night after treating myself to some time with my hand and thoughts of Sidney Blount. Specifically Sidney Blount's long fingers, maybe even still clad in those tight leather gloves.

I came so hard I had to bite the pillow to keep from groaning.

So I slept well and rose just after the light began filtering in. But even though it's early, even though the house is silent except for the wind and the hiss of snow on the windows, the library is not empty.

There's someone here.

Sidney Blount sits at one of the long tables stretching down the middle of the room, his toned frame hugged by a black turtleneck sweater and gray trousers. He's poring over a piece of paper, the fingers I thought so much about last night following a line of text as he reads. The snowy half-light coming in from the windows at the end of the library is faint enough that he has a lamp on the table, and the light casts the strong lines of his face into arresting plays of shadow and glow.

"Good morning, Ryan," he says without lifting his eyes from his paper.

My name on his lips is shocking, electric magic, and I nearly trip over my own feet.

"Good morning, Sidney," I choke out.

"Mr. Blount will do," he says crisply, finally turning to face me.

I flush with either indignation or shame . . . or both. "I—ah, okay?"

"Is that going to be a problem? Me calling you Ryan, while you call me Mr. Blount?"

I suppose it should be, but as I reflect on it, I find that it isn't. I'm used to it, after all. I've spent the last four years delivering every formality and courtesy to the people around me, and of course, it's expected in the world of kink that language and names acknowledge the power play between Dominants and submissives. Not that Sidney and I are playing a game like that now.

I think.

"It's not a problem if it's on purpose," I say.

"I would think it being on purpose would be worse."

"No, because you asked if it was okay and I'm telling you it's okay. If you didn't ask, if you didn't think about why you needed the honorific and I didn't, then I'd know not to trust you."

Sidney studies me for a moment, firm lips pressed into a thoughtful line. "Noted. And will it bother you if I work in here?" He gestures at the boxes and folders in front of him. "It's easier if I have room to spread out."

Spread me out instead. Work on me until I'm shivering and crying. Work on me until I beg for mercy.

"It won't bother me," I say, walking forward enough to set my mug at the edge of the table. I hope I look casual and collected, and not like I'm already planning to jerk off thinking about him again. "As long as it won't bother you that I'm in here?"

"Of course not. I overheard part of your conversation with Mr. Cremer yesterday, and I understand you're looking for a book?"

I can't tell if he's being polite or if he truly wants to know . . . until I meet his gaze, and then there's no mistaking his interest. His stare is keen and his eyebrow is arched, as if he's impatient with my hesitation in answering.

"Yes," I say. "*The Tragicall Story of Tristram and Iseult of Lyonesse.* There's only two copies known to history, and one was destroyed in Germany during the war. The other copy is possibly here."

"Possibly?"

"There's a letter from John William Waterhouse thanking an Estamond Guest for letting him peruse the library while he stayed here during a house party. He mentions finding the *Tragicall Story* deeply inspiring and that he'd love to paint the lovers, which he did many years later. However, the letter is from the 1870s and there's no hint of this book being here after that."

"And what is this book to you?"

"A job," I say honestly.

"Are you getting paid?"

"It's not that kind of job."

Sidney narrows his eyes. "And who is it that asks for this job? Who has enough loyalty from you to claim your time like this?"

"It's not—" my hands move a little helplessly, as if I can make the shape of the situation I'm trying to describe. "I think Merlin is trying to do me a favor. Give me a purpose. I've been a little . . . lost . . . after the President's death."

Sidney seems to relax a little at my answer. "Merlin . . . Merlin Rhys?"

"You know him?"

"Everyone knows him. Why do you think he wants this book?"

"It's really his Do—" I stop myself from saying the word *Domme*, switch to something else. "It's his girlfriend that wants it, really. She didn't say why. Just that they'd pay for me to come out here and fetch it."

"Mm," Sidney says, clearly cataloging all this away. "So you search the library until you find this book and you'll bring it back to Merlin, and then what?"

"I don't have another job lined up after this, if that's what you're asking."

"It is what I'm asking," he says, a bit tersely, and then turns back to his work.

I stare at him for a minute, a little stunned, and yet under the astonishment there's the feeling of an itch being scratched, the familiarity of a curt dismissal from a powerful man. It's so known to me, so recognizable, that I'm smiling a little as I head to the far corner of the library, where I plan to start my search for Tristram and Iseult. In a way, it's like working with Ash again.

THREE HOURS LATER, and my lack of success has only made me more determined. I've gotten through a good tenth of the shelves, but it's slow, tedious work, slower than I could have ever imagined. First of all, there's no real order to the library, no sections or classifications, or any kind of organizational scheme at all. There's no records, no catalogs, no metadata I can use to make my search any easier. And secondly, there's not enough light to see what the hell I'm doing. The snow has grown worse, thicker and faster, and even with a lamp dragged along behind me, the gloom is so thick that I have to use my phone flashlight to see.

And complicating it all is the aged state of the books themselves —some of them without titles on their spines, some with titles but with the lettering peeling off and rendering the title unrecognizable. I have to pull most books off the shelf and check the front page to see what they are, and it's so fucking time consuming.

I finish another row and pause to stretch, re-evaluating all the project flow-charts I'd made in my mind yesterday. People often think that being methodical and being efficient are synonymous, but that's not the case. Sometimes efficiency requires creativity rather than logic, it requires vision; I pride myself on seeing the shortcuts other people miss.

So I take a minute to examine the library once again, now that I'm more familiar with it. I take in the huge fireplace to one side, the dusty reaches of the upper story, the ladders and stairs giving access to high shelves and balconies in a baroque tangle of dark wood.

And of course, my gaze is pulled to the elegant arch of Sidney's neck over his mysterious papers, to the contrast of his strong, cut jaw against his black turtleneck. From this angle, the cashmere-covered planes of his shoulders and biceps are framed by the rows of richly colored books just beyond him, and—

Ah. Interesting.

On that same bookshelf in front of Sidney, I spy two large items that look more like ledgers than books. When I head over to investigate, I realize I'm going to have to climb the little ladder to reach them, and with a sigh I do, very aware that my jeans are not made for climbing things. With each rung, I can feel the denim pulling indecently tight around my ass and thighs. I just pray Sidney of the Impeccable Tailoring isn't looking at me right now.

"Do you need help?" he asks from behind me. He's gotten up and moved with such silent, catlike grace that I had no idea he was there.

"Um, I'm fine," I say, reaching for the books and trying to get myself down to where he can't see all the anatomical detail my jeans are currently revealing. But before I can take a single step down, Sidney's on the ladder behind me, reaching for the books in my hand.

"Don't move," he orders, and I don't move.

There's the light tap of his Derby shoes reverberating through the wood, the gone-too-soon press of him against my back, and then he has both books in his hand and is climbing back down.

The ghost of all that lean warmth keeps me frozen for a long second, long enough for him to say from the floor, with a touch of wry amusement, "Do you need help down?"

"No," I say quickly, not wanting him to see how much he affects me. "No, I'm completely fine."

"Hmm," he says, setting the ledgers on the table and going back to his work, and his *hmm* sounds like he's not entirely fooled by my act.

But just a moment later, when I'm moving the ladder back to where I found it, he lets out a ragged breath, and when I turn, he has his eyes closed and his hand in a fist on the table.

Like it's taking all of his control to remain right where he is.

5

"So these were Estamond's records?" Auden asks, as I set the books on the sofa next to him. It's after dinner, and the four of us have repaired to the library with whiskey to enjoy the big fireplace and the snow still fluttering past the windows in the dark.

"As far as I can tell. It doesn't look like she got anything close to having the whole library surveyed, but some of it is here."

Auden flips through the brittle pages, eyes running over lines and lines of browned, century-old ink. "Fascinating."

Sidney, who's standing at the arm of the sofa and looking down over Auden's shoulder, moves away to the window. The firelight in the shadowy room dances everywhere, dances over the subtle lines of muscle and spine on his cashmere-covered back. "I still think you should consider hiring someone to take care of this," he says as he goes.

Auden doesn't look up from the amateur library catalog. "I don't even know what that means," he says. "I'm not sure if I care."

"You could at least finish Estamond's work and properly catalog the library," Cremer says from the far sofa across the coffee table. "You could even arrange for the digitization of books that haven't been digitized in other libraries yet. Think about it, Auden. If that

Tristram and Iseult is the only copy left in the world and it's *here*, how many other rare things are held hostage in Thornchapel's walls?"

It's the boldest I've ever heard Cremer speak, and I suspect it has something to do with how little scotch is left in his glass.

Auden must notice too, because he looks up at his lawyer with one of those boy-king smiles he has. "Cremer, you *are* saucy tonight! And about books, of all things!"

My phone buzzes in my pocket, and when I pull it out, I see a message from a number I don't recognize.

Unknown number: This is Nimue. Tell Mr. Cremer to hire a woman named Proserpina Markham to work on Thornchapel's library.

I stare at the phone for a long time, not really sure what I'm seeing. But four years working with Merlin has left me resigned to these sorts of things—when magic crops up, it's always more work to ignore it than to let it blow through your life. With a sigh, I turn to Cremer.

"You should hire someone named Proserpina Markham," I say very quickly, hoping it sounds less bonkers if I blurt it out.

The ledger Auden holds falls shut with a loud, papery *clap*. I glance over at him in surprise, even more surprised to see a muscle ticking wildly in his jaw.

"What did you just say?" he whispers. His long eyelashes sweep over those hazel eyes like dark fans as he looks at me with something like shock. "What name did you just say?"

"Proserpina Markham," I repeat. "It's a mouthful, I know."

Auden is staring at me hard enough to etch my skin with his questions. My phone buzzes again.

Nimue: She's a rare book archival specialist in the U.S.

"She's an archival specialist," I parrot.

Auden shoves the ledgers off his lap to stand. "Holy fuck," he mutters to himself. He spears long fingers through his light brown hair in jerky, agitated movements. "Holy *fuck*."

I take a look at my pacing host and then at the tipsy lawyer in front of me, who already looks eager to pounce on whatever this means to Auden if it will result in Auden hiring a librarian, and I quietly excuse myself from the seating area. I probably should get myself another drink or pretend to sift through the ledgers some more—polite, meaningless activity while I give Auden and Cremer privacy—but I can't help it, I'm drawn to the giant windows.

I'm drawn to the tall, wide-shouldered man silhouetted against the glass.

Sidney stands with one hand in a pocket and the other with his scotch glass dangling between his fingertips. He's gazing out at the snow-beleaguered scene outside, but he nods when I come to stand next to him, as if he's been aware of my movements the whole time.

"Ryan." He takes a drink.

"Mr. Blount."

We share a quiet moment together, just watching the snow come down and the laden trees creak in the wind. Then he says, abruptly, "Your President. Did you love him?"

There's no sense in lying. "Yes."

His fingers tighten around the glass. "Were you lovers?"

"No. Why are you asking?"

"Because, Ryan Belvedere, I want to know what I'm up against."

Shock and hope thud through my bloodstream; I have to swallow before I speak. "What you're up against?"

Sidney takes a step forward, close enough that I can see the reflection of the firelight glinting in his eyes. "Yes," he says quietly. "Am I competing with the hero you gave your body to, or only your heart? Have I lost the chance to try for you before I've even met you?"

I don't think I can breathe. "Mr. Blount..."

Another step forward. "You didn't shave today," he murmurs. "It makes me want to touch your jaw. Is that a problem?"

And I finally get it, finally get that when he asks *is this a problem*, he's actually asking if it's okay, he's asking if he *can*.

He's asking for consent.

That realization sends a hot frisson of need right to my dick. "It's not a problem," I say hoarsely.

And he touches my jaw.

His fingers are warm and probing over my stubbled skin, and his stare is so intense that I can barely endure it. He traces along the bone from my ear to my chin, and then he takes my chin between his fingers, searching my face.

"So you weren't lovers?"

"I never slept with the President, no."

Sidney hears the subtext in my carefully chosen words, and his mouth flattens. "What does that mean?"

"He sent me to his former Vice President. As a . . . gift. Only once."

"Hmm. Did you love the Vice President too?"

For the first time, I'm able to say it out loud. "Yes. I loved him. And I loved Ash. I loved his wife too. I loved them all, I wanted to be with them all."

"And now? Do you pine for Embry Moore and Greer Colchester even as you grieve for your President?"

I take a deep breath, staring into Sidney's firelight eyes, feeling his warm fingers gripping me. It feels safe. It feels beautiful.

Beautiful enough to let go of something I've held onto for too long. "No," I say. "I don't pine for them. And Ash—I grieve and I mourn, but maybe I can . . ."

I trail off. I don't know what words I want, I don't know what words I mean. How can I explain that I'll always mourn Ash, but that right here—tonight, with the snow swirling and the firelight flickering in this cathedral of books, tonight with Sidney's cruel mouth and conqueror's eyes—I'm ready to set the mourning aside? That I'm willing to consider something new?

Some*one* new?

Sidney's fingers tighten once and then he releases my chin. So he can take my hand.

It's such a simple touch. The warmth of fingers interlacing and palms pressing in a cold room. And yet because it's him, because it's this sharp-edged ice god touching me, I feel his touch everywhere. Skating over the furrow of my spine and teasing at the creases of my knees and thighs. Brushing over my nipples and ghosting over secret places no one's touched in months and months.

My cock, which was gradually stirring in his presence, is now so hard that I know he'll be able to tell if he looks down, even in the dim room.

"I want to be the one, Ryan," he says in that crisp, elegant voice of his. "The one you begin to try with, and the one you open up to. I want you to be mine, like you were his."

My heart is hammering so hard that I feel like everyone in the room must be able to hear it, even as my brain tumbles over and over trying to parse his words. "You want me to be yours, like I was his," I repeat slowly.

What does that even mean? He wants me to be his aide? He's offering a job? Or he wants me to love him and serve him, but not share my body?

Sidney bends his head slightly so that our eyes meet again. "Do you understand what I'm asking?"

"No, Mr. Blount." If he wants to hire me, then why hold my hand? If he wants me to serve him like I served Ash, then why are his eyes dropping to my mouth even now, as if he's already making plans for it?

He blows out a breath. "I've phrased this badly. I shouldn't have brought his memory into it—but I couldn't help it. I'm jealous of him." His mouth twists at the corner with irony. "I'm jealous of a dead man. I'm jealous of how faithful you are to his memory when you didn't even fuck, and I'm jealous that he had the use of your body at all, even if it was only to give it to someone else. I want that right. I want that faithfulness."

Our hands are still held tight, and he puts his glass to his mouth with his other hand, taking a sip of scotch. I'm about to do the same with mine, just to do anything, perform any gesture that makes this surreal moment real, but he shakes his head and lifts *his* drink to my lips instead. The glass is cool, the whisky rich, and when I part my lips to accept it, his eyes darken with pleasure.

It's so erotic to be fed like this, given something from a powerful man's glass and at his hand, and it's so sexy that I don't even care that we're not shrouded from view, that Auden and Cremer could look over here at any time and see us holding hands, see us sharing this moment.

Sidney doesn't seem to care either, because when I finish drinking, he lowers the glass to the stone windowsill and then uses a thumb to wipe the wet trace of whisky from my lips. And then he puts his thumb to his own mouth and licks it off.

I nearly slump against the window.

"I don't want you to be my aide," he says, giving his thumb a final dart with his tongue. "I don't need a servant, and I don't want you to be either of those things for me, at least not in the way that you have been in the past. When you serve me, when you act as my squire, it will be a choice and a game we play. I want to be your master and your only king, I want you to belong in my keeping, I want to fuck you and to care for you and to learn about you and share your time and your body and maybe your heart after enough time has passed. Is that a problem?"

Which means *can I?*

He can. If he's asking what I think he's asking.

"It's only been two days," I say, as I consider what I *really* want to say. What I really want to ask.

"I don't need longer," he says with an arrogant lift of his head. "I want you."

"And do you have anybody else in your keeping?"

"Do you think I'd be spending my Christmas sorting through art provenance papers if I did?"

"Why isn't there anyone else, then?"

He lets out a long breath. "Because I'm cruel and I'm cold, and sometimes I like to make the people I love cry. Any other questions?"

"Yes," I say. "We haven't put a name to this . . . we haven't said the words. But I've only ever done this before in a formal setting."

"In a club, you mean."

"Right. I've never done this in real life. I've never had a Dominant who was mine for more than a session, I've never had a man who wanted my heart *and* my pain."

Sidney's eyes look impossibly tender. "Never? You are so young."

"And you're not," I say. "You've done this before? You know how it works?"

"You mean, have I had men that I took to the movies and out to dinner and that I also flogged and humiliated? Yes."

Now I think I'm a little jealous. How ridiculous that we should be jealous of each other's pasts when we've known each other for less than forty-eight hours, and yet . . . I can't lie to myself. The jealousy is invigorating, it's potent and intoxicating. It feels like being alive, wanting what I can't have, wanting total and complete occupation in the heart of a near-stranger.

"You'll find that it's not so different," Sidney says. "The club and real life. You'll tell me your limits, and you'll tell me what gets you hard. You'll tell me what you desire most and what you'll do to earn it . . . tell me how far I can go, and tell me what you expect in return. And then we'll begin."

"And when I find the book and have to leave?"

His hand tightens on mine, as if he's already trying to keep me from leaving. "You don't have to go, you know. Not if you don't want."

"Mr. Blount."

"What has you so eager to return?" he asks. "If there's not a job or a lover waiting, then why not tarry with me?"

I don't have a good answer to that. The truth is that after four years of doing nothing but attending to someone else's needs, I have plenty of savings and no real urgency to find another situation. The lease on my tiny D.C. studio is up next month and I still haven't decided what to do about it. My life is as shapeless as candle smoke right now.

The interesting thing is that Sidney's offer makes my candle-smoke life seem like a *good* thing, an *exciting* thing, as opposed to the burden it felt just a day ago.

I feel free instead of lost.

"I'd need a place to stay."

"You could stay with me," he says, and I know the caution in his voice is because he doesn't want to spook me. "I have plenty of space, plenty of room."

"You'd want me to stay with you?"

He tilts his head. "Does that bother you?"

"I don't know." The words are uncomfortable in my mouth.

I'm just like everyone else: I grapple with uncertainty, nuance, ambiguity. The only difference is that for the last four years, I wasn't allowed to say *I don't know*, I was always expected to have the answer. Or to find the answer as fast as possible. It feels oddly good to say it again, the initial discomfort disappearing into the soothing power of the words. "I don't know."

"You don't have to know," Sidney assures me. "As long as you tell me when you do."

"And until then?"

"Until then, I want to guide us. I want to lead us. Is that a problem?"

"No," I whisper. "It's not a problem."

6
_____

Sidney wants to wait until the next day to start, much to my painful, physical frustration. Every part of it, from holding hands to him licking his thumb for the mingled taste of whisky and my mouth, has me so hard that walking back to my room is uncomfortable, much less showering and trying to sleep.

But like any good sadist, he wants me to choose his cruelty with a clear mind and after a full night's sleep.

"Anyone might say yes like this," he told me before we rejoined the others. He gestured to the snow and the fire and the books. "It's easy to say yes like this."

Meaning, I suppose, that it's harder to choose pain and shame while the sun is shining on every crack and flaw in the room. I admire his caution, although I admire it less as I burn alone between my sheets because, of course, his only prohibition as my provisional Dominant was to forbid me to come.

Dammit.

Luckily, the specter of Proserpina Markham, whoever she was, had Auden so agitated last night that he and Cremer seemed wholly unaware of what Sidney and I shared by the window, and when I bump into Auden in the kitchen this morning, he seems distracted and not at all like he suspects I'm going to his library to be spanked by his art surveyor.

"Everything okay?" I ask as I get some water. I'm too nervous for coffee and I'd rather wait to eat until after Sidney's used my body.

The young master of the house just pulls on his hair a little. "Everything's fine." He gives me a forced smile. "I'm fine."

"Ah. Okay. Let me know if I can help with anything?"

"No one can help," he murmurs, as if to himself. And then he tries a cheerful change of subject. "Should be a quiet day. Cremer left early to get to London, even though the roads are still terrible, and the weather's too awful for the renovation work to continue. I'm planning on holing up in my study all day to work, if you need me for anything."

"And you're not going back to London for Christmas?"

"My parents are dead," Auden says bluntly, so bluntly that I almost miss the glimpse of shy pain in his eyes. "And the rest of my life is . . . complicated. I think I'm just going to stay here and go to Mass."

"Mass?" I say. I didn't expect to encounter another Catholic out here in the British countryside. "Are you Catholic?"

Another forced smile. "Also complicated."

"Ah."

I want to ask him more, I want to ask him about Proserpina Markham and why his life is so complicated, but I also really, really want to be alone with Sidney. So I take my water and take my leave.

The narrow corridor leading to the library is lined with arched windows—one side facing the front of the house and the driveway, and the other facing an inner courtyard with some lonely benches and a fountain. Everything is blanketed in storybook bluffs of snow, thick and white and blinding.

But there's no storybook prince behind this door. Only a man with a snow-cold heart and a voice like ice.

I can't wait.

When I push inside, Sidney is predictably already at work. Today he's in another turtleneck and trousers, but his sleeves are pushed to his forearms and I can see a large watch glint on his wrist. Next to him on the table are a bottle of water and a necktie. And next to those are his leather gloves, their presence both playful and ominous.

"Close the door, Ryan," Sidney says without looking up from his work. "And put those door wedges against the inside of the doors so they can't be opened from the outside. Then come here."

Last night, he came to my bedroom after everyone retired to bed, and he sat in the corner chair and made me answer all kinds of sordid questions. Did I like spanking? Whipping? Bondage? Did I like to crawl and beg? How did I like to be praised? How noisy was I when I came? What were the things I imagined when I jerked off that I didn't want anybody to ever, ever know about? Could I describe them in better detail? Would I move forward into the light so he could see my ashamed blushes as I did?

We talked for nearly two hours, deciding on the common green-yellow-red system of safe wording, since Sidney admitted that he's not unaroused by discomfort and protests, and this would allow him to enjoy the occasional plea for mercy while still giving me a way to safe out. And we also decided on an adaptable but mostly full-time arrangement . . . at least for the next couple of days. After spending so many years as a body man, I find the idea of moving from power exchange to normal lover time and back again unnerving. I'd rather stick to the former and then have some grace and flexibility around the edges.

So I already know as I approach him that I'll be safe, that he won't demand of me anything I'm not willing to give, and I can be present in the moment. I can be horny and vulnerable and excited and nervous and ready.

I can just be me.

"I'd like to work by the fireplace," Sidney says once I reach him. He still doesn't bother to look at me. "Will you carry my work over to the wingback chair?"

He's uncomfortably beautiful from this angle. His hands, large but sophisticated, look like a lover's hands. The tip of his strong nose is caught with the morning light while shadows gather in the tiny well in at the top of his upper lip. He's the kind of beautiful Ash was, the kind Embry and Greer and even Auden Guest are; it's the kind of beauty that compels devotion not because it's visually flawless but because it promises untold mysteries beyond itself. The beauty is only a gate, a threshold to a secret inner world only a privileged few ever get to see.

I arrange Sidney's work into batched piles, which I stack in perpendicular sections so he won't lose any of the organization he's done. I can see that he notices this and is pleased by my care, and that has me smiling as I set it all on the table next to the chair and go back for his pen and iPad.

He's sitting when I return, his firm lips pressed together in fresh unhappiness. "It's not as comfortable as I'd hoped."

"I'll get you a pillow for your back, Mr. Blount." Which is ridiculous, since a man as fit as Sidney doesn't really need a pillow for his back, but it doesn't matter *why* I'm moving around the room at his beck and call, only that I *am*. It's all part of the game we decided on last night, and it's almost unnerving how quickly the game relaxes me, even as it arouses me.

The pillow's fetched, and then Sidney decides he's too chilled, and makes me light a fire for him. And then he's thirsty. And then he's too warm after all and wants me to angle the chair away from the flames.

"I think I've finally found the reason I'm not comfortable," Sidney says after a moment. "I need a footstool. Could you find me one, please?"

Only in Sidney's voice could politeness sound nothing like politeness. The *please* only underscores the command that came before it, the slight touch of condescension making it clear that every courteous or genteel moment I have with him is an allowance given only at his pleasure, and I have no right to expect or demand otherwise.

That coolly uttered *please* is like leather stroking down my back. I want to purr.

Despite the scatter of plush leather and damask seating around the fireplace, the library is quite bereft of anything that would make a decent footstool. The wooden chairs around the long tables would be too high and the coffee table nearby would be too low. And even though I knew where this little play was leading the whole time, I still feel a shiver of foreboding and excitement when I think *it'll have to be me.*

I dressed in jeans and a cardigan today, figuring my nerd-casual look would serve the dual purpose of being comfortable and also underscoring the difference in power between me and Sidney in all his restrained polish. I try not to be embarrassed when I again feel the jeans pull tight around my ass and thighs as I get to my knees and lower my head to the ground. I try to remain calm as I curl myself into a serviceable footstool and hear Sidney's murmur of pleasure.

The snow has amplified the daylight into startling brightness. Even down on the rug with my head hanging between my shoulders, I can see all the individual twists and fibers, the places under the chairs that a vacuum missed, a forgotten wine cork, the bit of dried cuticle on my left thumb. How strange to see everything with the harsh and rational sobriety of day . . . and then still to feel a man's shoes settle onto my back. Still to feel the heels of them digging into my skin, still to strain against my jeans with a needy erection at the shame of it all.

"You are a good footstool, Ryan," Sidney says calmly. I can hear but not see the flipping of papers, the occasional tap of a finger on his iPad as he wakes it up to take notes or snap a quick picture of what-ever document he's reading. I wonder if I'm in the pictures; I wonder if you looked hard enough you'd see the curve of a man's back under the expensive leather of Sidney's shoes.

Running after Ash for four years—sometimes running *with* him if he decided he didn't want to exercise alone that day—means I'm not unfit, but the position gets difficult fast. Even on my elbows, the weight of Sidney's legs is enough to start my arms trembling. My cock is pinioned between my hip and my jeans in such a way that even the slightest shift in position is agony. And once Sidney sees I'm suffering, he adds to it for his amusement, pressing down harder with his legs, digging the soles of his shoes deeper into the muscles of my back.

We play this game for so long that I have sweat misting my face, even in this chilly room, and when he finally lifts his feet off my back, I'm breathing hard enough that my sides are heaving.

But I don't get up. Not yet. Not without his express permission. There's already going to be pain today, and while I'm a sucker for pain, there's no sense in bringing more wrath down on my head because I couldn't be patient.

"So well trained," Sidney murmurs above me. "I'm envious of whoever got the pleasure of breaking you in. What was their name?"

"Mark," I say. "At a club called Lyonesse in D.C. He trained Ash as well."

Then I shut up, because I'm not so sure it's a good idea to strum the strings of jealousy just now.

"Hmm," Sidney says in that way of his. And then he sighs. "I'm still not comfortable, Ryan."

"I'm sorry to hear that, Mr. Blount."

"Get on your knees and face me."

He lifts his feet and I do, kneeling between his legs and looking up into his imperious face. I've knelt countless times at the club, in front of Mark or some other Dominant willing to play with me, but the difference between kneeling in a dark club and in a bright library is vast. And kneeling in front of someone who I eventually want to eat pizza with and whose childhood pictures I'd like to see is also unnerving. If I fail to please him here, what does that mean outside these walls? Would he be so eager for me to come to London and stay with him if I don't satisfy him here, now?

Sidney's eyes are perceptive and searching on my face, and he reaches forward to run a finger along my jaw. "I can see the worry in you," he says. His voice is still cool and clipped, but there's something gentle in it too. He's being kind—or at least as kind as he's capable of being. "You've already made me very happy. Would you like to see?"

"Yes, Mr. Blount," I breathe, and he dips his head to his lap in permission.

"Then look for yourself."

I raise my hand—tentative, still not sure if I'm allowed—and run my palm along his thigh. It's the first I've gotten to touch him, and it's like the first bite into an apple—punctured anticipation and the explosion of sweetness after.

I could not have imagined it would feel so good to touch him. I could not have imagined the warm sculpture of his firm leg under my hand, or the faint quiver of his body under my touch, proving that he's just as affected by this moment as me. I couldn't have known that brushing one hand up his clothed thigh would be enough to make me shudder. If I weren't already on my knees, I'd be falling to them now.

Other than the repressed quiver of his muscles and the finger still toying idly with my jaw, Sidney stays completely still as my hand reaches the thickness currently stretching all the way out to his hip. He stays completely still as I explore the impressive length of him, the swollen crown all plump and distended, the wide base and the convexity of his testicles underneath.

He drops his hand to cover mine, moves it to the fly of his trousers. "Don't just feel. I told you to look."

"At where you're happy?"

"And at where I'm uncomfortable," he says, arching an eyebrow enough to tell me we're back to business.

I unbutton his trousers, wondering how an action that I do several times a day can be so clumsy when I'm doing it with someone else. And then I cease to wonder anything at all as I part his zipper and see his naked, erect cock.

It's thicker than I originally thought, and long enough to rest obscenely against the cashmere covering his most of his torso. There's a light, masculine fur of hair on his lower belly, and the crisp hair around his root has been kept neat. It's the cock of a calculating and fastidious man—but an arrogant one too. Even the way it juts up from his groin and beads with precum at the tip seems vain and demanding. Just like Sidney himself.

"If you put your mouth on it," he says. "I might feel better."

I glance up at him through my lashes, just to confirm, and whatever he sees in my face has him fisting his hand in my hair.

"Fuck, you're pretty," he hisses through his teeth, yanking my face down to his waiting erection. "You know what I thought when I first saw those eyelashes? Those pretty, dark eyes of yours? That I couldn't wait to have you on your knees, just like this, looking up at me through those doll's eyelashes while I fed you my cock."

"Yes, Mr. Blount," I moan. And he does as he says and pushes himself past my lips and into my waiting mouth. I make sure to look up at him, catch his gaze as he rubs himself against my tongue. His eyes are hooded, burning on mine, and if I was nervous earlier about pleasing him, it's all gone now. There can be no doubt that he wants me, that he'll want me again after. I'm even better than the Roman artifacts in the glass cases; he's appraised me and now he wants to keep me.

He's clean, soap-scented, with just the barest trace of salt to his taste, and I moan again as I manage to take him deeper, into the tight clench of my throat.

"Ah, again," he says, using the fingers twisted in my hair to force the issue. His hips thrust up as he pulls me down, and soon he's fucking my throat with just enough consideration for my breathing that I don't pass out—but not so much care that I don't have tears streaming fast and hard down my face.

"Those tears," he grunts, and I know what he sees. I know he sees them glinting on the long fans of my eyelashes. I know the bright sunlight pouring in through the windows must be making them sparkle. "Fuck, Ryan. Those tears."

And then he comes. Pulsing, thick, hot—all down my throat, all while his cruel hand forces me down against him. My own cock throbs in response, it aches. It keens. I think I might be able to come too if I swivel my hips just right to rub my tip against the inside of my jeans, but I don't even get the chance to try because Sidney stands up and hauls me to my feet, even as I'm still swallowing the very last of his spend.

He doesn't bother to zip himself up—instead he leaves himself exposed, still mostly hard and still wet from my mouth—as he drags me over to the long library table.

"Wrists out," he says, in a tone that brooks no argument.

Not that I would argue.

My wrists are tied quickly, with the expertise of someone who's done it countless times before, and he checks my circulation with the detached efficiency of a nurse. Then my jeans are unbelted, the leather making a slow, sinister hiss as it slides from my loops, and my jeans are unbuttoned and unzipped.

Sidney tugs the waist of them down and my cock hits the cool air, finally free to throb and swell as much as it wants, and I make an involuntary noise when I see his hand move up, like he's going to touch me.

"Please, Mr. Blount," I say when his hand moves away. It's everything I can do not to start crying again. "Please."

"Please what?" he asks indifferently. He's already turning toward the table, towards the other things he laid out for us today.

"Please t-touch me."

"Touch you? You mean touch your cock?"

"Yes, Mr. Blount."

"And make you come? Is that what you want? That's a very selfish thing to want, by the way."

"I know, Mr. Blount, but please."

"It does look like it hurts an awful lot," he observes as he reaches for his leather gloves and starts pulling them on. "Does it? Hurt?"

"Yes," I whimper, my eyes on his hands. Those gloves—the gloves I asked for last night because it turned me on so much to think about being handled by him while he wore them. It feels like all of the blood in my body has gone to my groin, like there's a fist at the base of my spine just squeezing and squeezing and squeezing. I'm terrified I'm going to erupt all over myself without even being touched.

"How about this?" Sidney suggests in a silky voice. He has his gloves on and my belt in one hand. "Let's trade one hurt for another."

Oh God, please don't let me come right now, please let me hold out. Please, please, please.

Sidney hikes up my cardigan so that my entire ass is exposed. The leather glove brushes against the skin at the small of my back and I shudder. "What color are we on, Ryan?" he asks.

"Green," I answer.

And a second later, the belt stripes leather-thick pain across my ass.

"And now?" Sidney inquires calmly.

"Green."

Another stripe. Another green. After the fourth strike, he stops asking, although he pauses between a couple to give me a moment to speak if I need to. I don't need to, even though I am crying by the tenth stroke, and my cock is so hard that it hurts too, and everything hurts and I'm dizzy and breathless.

He drapes the belt over a chair and comes to stand behind me.

"Still green?" he asks gently.

"Yes," I mumble. "Green."

A cool leather hand fists my organ, and I gasp, my knees nearly buckling. But Sidney is right behind me, strong and tall and sure, his fully erect cock nestled against my welted ass as he grips me and begins to stroke. I slump against him.

"I got you," he says in my ear. His hand on me is tight and mean, and so, so, so good. He jerks me like I need, he jerks me fast and hard and without mercy, jerks me with those leather gloves I've been thinking so many filthy things about. The friction is vicious, and there's a bite to the bliss he's giving me, but I don't even care. I'd rather have this from him than undiluted pleasure from anyone else.

"You can come for me," he says. His cock burns hot and hard against my ass as he grinds himself closer. "You've earned it, haven't you? Haven't you earned it?"

Fuck, *fuck*, I have, I have earned it—it's all I want, to make the people around me happy and better and to earn all the good things I want—

My back bows as raw, primal release scissors up from out of me. Something deep in my groin is flexing, pumping, even as my cock flexes and pumps on the outside, spurting seed all over Sidney's fist and onto the table, more and more and more until I'm shaking and drained and everything is incandescent, electric sensation. Pleasure, pain, bliss and ache—everything, everything.

Sidney's lips are on my neck as I gradually come down, and like the pleasure he gave me earlier, the sweet sensation of his mouth is threaded through with the sting of pain as he nips at my flesh. Then I feel him laughing against me, the vibrations of his laughter sending delicious tingles through his lips to my throat.

It's the first time I've heard him laugh.

"What's so funny?" I ask, realizing I sound drunk. I also realize I don't care. It feels too good to be like this, warm and beaten against such a stern, handsome man. Even if he's not so stern right now.

"I came again," he says, still laughing a little. "All over you. Like an adolescent."

He's right, and now that I'm coming down a little, I can feel it, slick and growing sticky where his pelvis is still slowly grinding against my ass.

"Don't feel bad," I say, smiling myself.

"Why would I feel bad? It was your fault for getting me so worked up." And with a final bite to my throat, Sidney unties me and together we go about the business of getting cleaned up.

7

That night, we fuck by the light of the small fire in Sidney's room. Because our rooms are so close to Auden's, I'm gagged, and Sidney amuses himself by scratching his nails over the still-raised welts from earlier and listening to me whimper. I'm also blind-folded, although there's no real reason for that—no reason other than that Sidney wants it and I want to give Sidney what he wants.

Sidney fucks like he does everything else—with cool, ruthless grace. He takes me on his bed, with me on my stomach and my head pillowed on my arms, and just before he comes into his condom, he flips me over and pulls down both the blindfold and the gag to my neck.

"Just wanted to see those pretty doll eyes," he breathes. And then he orgasms with a gorgeous sigh, the firelight revealing the clenching, glistening muscles of his belly as he fills the latex with his seed.

It's enough of a sight to send me right to the edge, and I am writhing against the air as he pulls out.

"Mr. Blount," I beg. He's gotten up to throw away the condom, and he comes back to the bed with a wicked look on his face.

"For the next fifteen minutes, I want you to call me Sidney," he says, and without further preamble, he dips his head and sucks my needy cock right into his mouth.

"Mr—*Sidney*," I gasp, trying to buck deeper into him. "Oh my God, Sidney, oh my God—"

I haven't felt a mouth on my cock since college, haven't felt the heat or the suction or the brush of someone's jaw against my thighs as they adjust their position in years. My toes curl, my back arches, and then Sidney looks up at me through *his* eyelashes, and I can see why he likes it so much, why it's such an erotic sight. There's something about the faux-demureness of the angle, the vulnerability of it. Innocence and mischief peering up while you compel them to service the rudest parts of you.

And that it's *Sidney*—sophisticated, arrogant *Sidney*—with his lips wrapped around me and his silver eyes glinting with amused power —it drives the pleasure of the act past what I can bear.

I ejaculate into his mouth with a soft, ragged noise, forcing myself to watch every single second of him swallowing me down. He lets me finish completely—he takes every pulse of me until I'm entirely spent, and then he arranges us on the bed so that we're laying side by side, with my head pillowed on his shoulder.

We were mostly clothed today, and I had my blindfold on for most of tonight, so I revel in simply getting to look at my new lover by firelight, spread out in a delicious length of muscle and dark hair.

"Can I touch you?"

He turns to me, his hair ruffled and his cheeks still splotched with exertion, and his expression the loose and satisfied look of a man who's had his needs tended to. "I'd like that," he says, and indeed, he does seem to like it. He likes when I stroke my fingers along the corrugations of his belly and when I explore the wide planes of his chest. He watches me with glittering, approving eyes when I press my lips to his nipples and explore the damp well of his navel with a darting tongue. And I get a very male purr when I tuck my mouth against the curves of his testicles and suck and lick until I've memorized their topography.

In fact, he likes me touching him so much that I end up getting fucked again, and neither of us can last much longer than it takes for him to get inside me and for me to grip my cock. We come, we clean up, and we fall asleep the way I've wanted to fall asleep for years—tucked safely into a master's arms, sleepy and welted and adored.

I FIND the book two days after Christmas. It's a slim volume tucked between two different amateur histories of Thornchapel, and it crackles ominously when I take it into my hands.

Sidney—who I've learned over the past few days is uncannily attuned to my movements—is up and peering over my shoulder at the book in seconds.

"Is that it?" he asks, and then takes it into his sure, expert hands once I've nodded. He examines it thoughtfully for a few moments.

"I've never heard of this publisher," he says, pointing to the title page. "And these endsheets are beyond luxurious. This must have been a very expensive book to own."

I search in vain for a date on the front. "How old do you think it is?"

"Books aren't my area of expertise," he says, frowning down as though it's the book's fault he spent years studying paintings instead. "But it looks mid-eighteenth century to me. Maybe a decade or two older."

He hands to book back to me with a "*hmm.*"

"'Hmm,' what, Mr. Blount?"

"*Tristram and Iseult of Lyonesse?* Wasn't your kink club called Lyonesse?"

I look down at the book, surprised. "It was. I mean, it is. What an interesting coincidence." Although even as I say the word *coincidence*, I somehow know it's got to be more than that. With Merlin, it always is.

Sidney puts me in touch with a company who can courier such a valuable item to Merlin, who is not in America, as I thought, but in Wales on some kind of romantic getaway with Nimue. And although we've spent the last four days in a heady fog of punishment, sex, and faking polite, disinterested conversation whenever Auden Guest is around, I do feel a bolt of trepidation as I sign the book over to the delivery service. I really no longer have a reason to intrude on Auden's hospitality, and what I have with Sidney feels too delicate to force into real life. I'm suspended in an awful limbo as I walk back from the front door to the library, and that limbo becomes hellish when I get to the library and see that Sidney is packing up boxes of provenance papers.

"Oh," I say. Stupidly. "Are you finished?"

"I've done all I can do here on site," he explains, settling a lid over one box and reaching for another. "I've examined the paintings them-selves and examined the documentation. I'll do the rest of the work at my office."

For four years, I've held my ground in front of generals and kings, and yet, right now, I want twist my hands in my sweater and plead.

Of course Sidney notices this, because those cold, perceptive eyes miss nothing, and he lets go of the box to walk over to me and take my face in his hands.

"You didn't know earlier, but I'm asking if you know now. Will you come to London with me? Will you allow me to try to win you?"

"Mr. Blount," I say, trying to duck my face. He doesn't let me. "I think you've already done that. Won me, I mean."

Sidney Blount, ice god and art expert, lets out a long, relieved sigh. "Thank fucking God."

I decide right then and there, when he's at his most vulnerable and his most human. Had I felt like I was drifting before I came to Thornchapel? That nothing would ever matter again?

How could I have been so wrong? When all this time I'd been drifting right towards him?

And then I have to wonder, *really* wonder, why Merlin had to send *me* to get this book. Why not come himself, if he's already in Wales? Why not have Cremer arrange for someone?

Could Merlin have known that I needed to meet Sidney Blount? Could he have constructed this entire scenario just to see me happy?

Maybe I am lucky to know a real wizard. Maybe I'm the luckiest man alive.

"I'm going to come with you," I declare.

Sidney's forehead drops to mine and his eyes sweep closed. "Oh, Ryan," is all he says.

"But what next?" I ask. "When I come with you, what will we do?"

What I mean is where will I live? How will I find a job? How much right will I have to your time? But what he says is, "Well, next, I think that I'd like to fall in love with you."

I melt. I die. I want.

"Is that going to be a problem?" he whispers, lowering his mouth to mine.

Which means, *can I*?

Yes, dammit. He can.

"Yes," I whisper into his kiss. "Yes and yes and yes. And yes."

IF YOU LOVED THE WORLD OF THORNCHAPEL . . .

Auden Guest's story is just getting started...

When librarian Poe Markham takes the job at Thornchapel, she only wants two things: to stay away from Thornchapel's tortured owner, Auden Guest, and to find out what happened to her mother twelve years ago. It should be easy enough—keep her head down while she works in the house's crumbling private library and while she hunts down any information as to why this remote manor tucked into the fog-shrouded moors would be the last place her mother was seen alive. But Thornchapel has other plans for her...

As Poe begins uncovering the house's secrets, both new and old, she's also pulled into the seductive, elegant world of Auden and his friends —and drawn to Auden's worst enemy, the beautiful and brooding St. Sebastian. And as Thornchapel slowly tightens its coil of truths and lies around them, Poe, Auden and St. Sebastian start unravelling into filthy, holy pleasure and pain. Together, they awaken a fate that will either anoint them or leave them in ashes...

***

From the author of the USA Today bestselling New Camelot series comes an original fairy tale full of ancient mysteries, lantern-lit rituals, jealousy, money, murder, sacred torment, and obsessions that last for lifetimes...

Learn More About A Lesson in Thorns and the Wild, Wicked Secrets of Thornchapel Here!

Want to know more about Ryan and the king he loved so dearly? Meet Maxen Ash Colchester in American Queen, the first in the New Camelot trilogy!

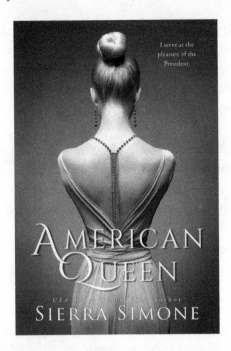

He wants me to be his queen...

Warned as a girl to keep her kisses to herself, Greer Galloway wants nothing to do with kisses--or love. Twice she's ignored the childhood warning and kissed a man, and both times ended in gutting, miserable heartbreak. Now she's sworn off all romance forever, determined to teach her classes and do her research, and live out the rest of her days alone.

I want to be his everything.

But Ash Colchester hasn't sworn off Greer--not at all. Still in love with the girl he once kissed in a circle of broken glass, this soldier-turned-President has never forgotten the taste of her kiss or the sound of her whispered, yes, please against his mouth. He's never forgotten the promises he wanted to make her and couldn't because she was too young for him then, and far too innocent for the things he needs. But he can't wait any longer . . .

But can a fairy tale have a happily ever after for three people?

Desperate to have her, Ash sends his best friend Embry to bring Greer to him, not knowing they have their own secrets, their own tragedies together. Their own cravings . . .

Soon, Greer finds herself caught between past and present, pleasure and pain--and the two men who long for each other as much as they long for her. And as war and betrayal press ever closer, they tumble headlong into a passionate love affair that will change the world.

My name is Greer Galloway and I serve at the pleasure of the President of the United States.

From the USA Today bestselling author of *Priest* and *Misadventures of a Curvy Girl* comes a contemporary reimagining of the legend of King Arthur, Guinevere, and Lancelot--elegant, carnal, and unforgettable.

Click here to enter the world of New Camelot!

ABOUT THE AUTHOR

Sierra Simone is a USA Today bestselling former librarian who spent too much time reading romance novels at the information desk. She lives with her husband and family in Kansas City.

Sign up for her newsletter to be notified of releases, books going on sale, events, and other news!

www.thesierrasimone.com
thesierrasimone@gmail.com

ALSO BY SIERRA SIMONE

Thornchapel:

A Lesson in Thorns

Feast of Sparks

Harvest of Sighs

Door of Bruises

Misadventures:

Misadventures with a Professor

Misadventures of a Curvy Girl

Misadventures in Blue (Coming September 2019)

The New Camelot Trilogy:

American Queen

American Prince

American King

The Moon (Merlin's Novella)

The Priest Series:

Priest

Midnight Mass: A Priest Novella

Sinner

Co-Written with Laurelin Paige

Porn Star

Hot Cop

The Markham Hall Series:

Printed in the USA
CPSIA information can be obtained
at www.ICGtesting.com
LVHW041359041023
760025LV00005B/444